NABUL, OUR LITTLE EGYPTIAN COUSIN

BLANCHE MCMANUS

Edition : Culturea (Hérault, 34)
Contact : infos@culturea.fr
Print in Germany by Books on Demand
Design and layout : Derek Murphy
Layout : Reedsy (https://reedsy.com/)
ISBN : 9791041819959
Légal deposit : July 2023

Nabul Our Little Egyptian Cousin

CHAPTER I

NABUL AND HIS LITTLE WHITE DONKEY

"HI-YAH! Hi-yah! Who will ride on Nabul's little donkey,—the swiftest donkey in all the great city of Cairo?" called out a shrill, clear voice. Through the crowded street there clattered a little white donkey and on his back was a small boy, laughing merrily and waving a short stick in one hand.

"Oh, look to thy face! Oh, look to thy heels! Oh, make way for me, good people!" cried the little boy as he guided his donkey skilfully through the crowd by taps with his heels.

As the donkey pushed his way along, everybody laughed good-naturedly, and stepped aside.

"'Tis only that imp of mischief, Nabul, and his donkey," they would say as they made way for the little rider, for everybody knew and liked little Nabul Ben Hassan, the youngest donkey boy in Cairo.

Presently the donkey trotted around a corner and nearly upset a little table of cakes, beside which sat an old man fast asleep. "Plague on thee, dost thou not yet know how to drive a donkey?" grumbled the old fellow, who woke up just in time to save his cakes.

"Nay, father, 'tis thou who knowst not how to sell cakes, for thou wast fast asleep, while the flies ate the sugar from thy cakes without paying for it," answered Nabul. This made the passers-by laugh, for Nabul was a great favourite in the quarter, and the old cake-seller was not, for sometimes he tried to cheat them when they came to buy his round, brown cakes covered all over with honey.

Nabul now hurried on the faster. He was anxious to reach the square where all the donkey boys of the city were to be found at noon, for he had a great piece of news to tell his chum Abdal, who would be sure to be there.

Nabul had just come from the big hotel in the main street where, along with all the other donkey boys, he liked to trot his little donkey up and down the street in front of the veranda, or terrace, of the hotel, hoping to attract the attention of those strange-speaking people who came from over the seas to see his country and to ride on the little Egyptian donkeys.

Indeed, truth to tell, the donkey boys thought the strangers came to Egypt just for that purpose, and out of compliment to the travellers, and with an eye to business, many of the boys named their donkeys after the great people of the various countries. There was a "King Edward" and a "Chamberlain" and a "Lord Cromer," to please the English, and another donkey was named after the French President "Fallieres," while Nabul himself called his "Teddy,"—you all know who that is,—and he usually called him "Teddy Pasha," because Pasha means, in his language, a great man.

Nabul already knew about America, that big country so far away, for did he not have an uncle who had been a "donkey boy" in "The Streets of Cairo" at the great Chicago Exposition, and was even now at a place called Coney Island? This uncle wrote him letters full of tales of wonderful doings, and did he not know also two of the oldest donkey boys now in Cairo who had been to the big Exposition in America?

Little Nabul never tired of listening to the marvellous tales they brought back with them, and in this way he came to know how to tell the Americans from the other strangers who visited Cairo, as he watched them sitting on the broad terrace of the hotel.

It was the Americans who laughed and joked the most with the little donkey boys. Often, too, if they happened to be in a very good humour, they would throw them milliemes, the smallest of Egyptian coins, and then such a scramble as went on among the boys down in the street as each tried to get a coin. This would only make the visitors laugh the more, when they would scatter more coins.

"What a country must be that from whence these strangers come," thought Nabul to himself, "that one can throw away money like that! How I should like to go there! Perhaps we will some day, Teddy Pasha. I won't go without thee," he went on, tapping the little donkey gently with his heels, as he sat proudly on his back. He was turning all this over in his mind to-day as he rode to find his cousin Abdal, who was most probably taking his midday rest with the other donkey boys.

When he reached the square it was noon. Here, in the shade of the locust and mimosa trees which bordered the square, stood dozens of donkeys of all sizes and colours,—white and brown and black and gray donkeys,—with bright-coloured saddles and blankets, and on their bridles and around their necks were strings of little jingling bells.

There are a great many donkeys in Egypt, for almost everybody uses a donkey on which to get about, and for that reason there are so many donkey boys who make a business of hiring out their clever little animals.

Some of the donkeys were fast asleep,—that is, they had their eyes tight shut, but one can never tell when a donkey is shamming; others were looking very wise out of the corners of their eyes, but it may have been that they were only planning how to dodge their work, or wondering if they could rub their saddles off against the tree-trunks, and thus give their young masters a little trouble. No one can possibly guess what a donkey is thinking about, though it is safe to say that Egyptian donkeys, like donkeys the world over, are generally up to mischief.

Meanwhile the young owners of the donkeys were stretched out on the ground in the shade. Some were playing a game like knuckle-bones; others were eating their lunch of honey cakes and dates, but all were chattering away at the top of their voices like so many magpies.

"Ho, here comes the little one!" they all cried out as Nabul rode up, sliding off his donkey and dropping down beside a boy a little older than himself. Meanwhile his little white donkey made at once for the bunch of his fellows and began pushing them about without ceremony, in order to make room for himself in the shade. This of course ended in a great braying and biting of ears, and the boys had to jump up and lay about them with their sticks before order was restored.

"Thy Pasha is like one possessed of an evil spirit," said one of the boys as he went back to his game.

"Nay, he is but masterful; see, he obeys one without the stick. Come here, little dove," called Nabul, who whistled to the little donkey who wriggled his long ears and came as meek as a lamb and stood by the side of his master.

"Abdal," said Nabul eagerly in a low voice to his companion lying in the shade, "I have good news for you. As I came by the big hotel I saw Mustapha, the dragoman, and he told me that it might be that he would want our donkeys to-morrow. There are two strangers at the hotel who have taken him for their dragoman. They have come from America in a big white ship to Alexandria, after many days on the ocean, and they are to stay a long time in our country. Mustapha is to be their guide, and if they want donkeys to ride Mustapha will see that they hire ours," and here Nabul paused for breath.

"Of a truth they will want donkeys, does not every one who comes to Cairo take a donkey ride through the bazaars and under the trees of the broad avenue leading out to the great pyramids?" demanded Abdal, sitting up and becoming as excited as his friend.

"Yes, but these strangers want to do more than that, for Mustapha says they may stay in our country for many weeks. One of these strangers is a boy like ourselves, and did you ever hear of a boy walking when he could ride?" asked Nabul triumphantly.

"But this boy may be different," said Abdal doubtfully; "however, if Mustapha has promised—"

"Well, he has," interrupted Nabul, "so to-morrow we must take care to be the first to show ourselves before them."

The two boys talked it over awhile longer as they ate their bread and dates and bit of cheese which they each took from a big pocket inside their long gowns. Abdal then ran across the square and bought a melon from a fruit merchant who sat there on a round, straw mat with his stock of melons heaped about him. After they had finished this the two cousins mounted and galloped away, each in a different direction.

Nabul and Teddy Pasha did some business that afternoon, carrying a few people up and down the busy streets in the centre of the city, but in such an absent-minded fashion on Nabul's part that he very nearly let the Pasha rub a fat old gentleman, who was riding him, off against a wall. The streets in the older part of Cairo are very, very narrow and crooked.

Usually it was quite dark when Nabul came home in the evening, but to-day he was anxious to tell the good news to his mother and the little sisters, so at sundown he and Teddy Pasha turned toward home.

As the little donkey trotted into the narrow street by the river where he and Nabul lived, Nabul's two little sisters came running to meet them. They had been watching for their brother as was their habit every evening, for often if he and Teddy were not too tired when they got home, they would be given a little canter to the end of the street and back, and they knew also that there were usually cakes or sweets in Nabul's pockets for them.

Nabul was very fond of his little sisters and good to them, better than little Egyptian boys often are to little girls; and as for the two little girls, they thought there was nobody in Cairo like their big brother.

The little girls were dressed in long blue cotton gowns and each wore a black veil wound around her head and hanging down to her waist. One of their greatest pleasures was to go out into the crowded city with Nabul, for they seldom went far away from their home by themselves.

This evening they hung close to their brother as he led Teddy into his stable, which was on the ground floor of the house. Nabul laughed as he caught Zaida peeping into his pocket. "Yes, I have brought thee a sweet morsel," he said, taking a little stick out of his pocket, on which were threaded a row of small cakes, "but I have brought you something better than sweetmeats, a piece of good fortune—maybe it may mean new dresses—who knows?" and he ran up the stairs laughing, with the little girls close behind and asking all sorts of questions.

Thus they tumbled into the big family living-room quite out of breath. "Thou makest noise enough for a small army, my children," said their mother, who was setting out the evening meal. "Thou art home early, my son, but all must be well, for thou art merry."

"He has a secret and will not tell it to us, mother," cried Menah, the eldest sister.

"Now you shall hear it, I waited to tell the mother first," said Nabul as he told his story of the strangers who wanted to engage two donkeys and their drivers for, as he hoped, many weeks.

"It would seem, indeed, to be the hand of good fortune which is held out toward thee," said the mother Mizram.

They all sat around on the floor, which was covered with matting, and Mizram gave each one a thin, flat sort of pancake made of corn meal well browned. This was their plate, and on it she heaped up a stew of mutton and big red peppers fried in oil. Children are never too happy nor too excited to eat, but between each mouthful they talked their prospects over and over again, and were only sorry to think that their father was not here, too, to hear the good news. Nabul's father, Mahomet Ben Hassan, was the captain of a dahabeah, an Egyptian sailing boat, which carried merchandise and native passengers up and down the river Nile. He was away now on a trip and would not be home again for a week or more. An Egyptianhousehold is very industrious, and every one of a suitable age and state of health is always very much occupied. Soon even the little girls would be taught to embroider, and their work would be sold to some merchant in the great Bazaar, and he in turn would sell it to strangers at, of course, a much higher price than the little girls would get for their labour.

When the girls had eaten the cakes that Nabul had brought them and some fruit, they sat in the big window that overlooked the river, and Abdal came in and sat with them until bedtime. Abdal's home was on a farm near Cairo, but since he had become a donkey boy he lived with friends just at the top of the street.

The little girls and their mother slept on a broad cot in the back room, up against the wall which was hung with matting to keep off the chill, but Nabul just rolled himself up in a woollen coverlid and slept on the hard matted floor, just as soundly, too, as he would have done in a soft bed.

As you may imagine, little Nabul did not oversleep the next morning. He was up with a bound as soon as he heard the call of the old muezzin from the little gallery of a near-by mosque, for that meant it was time for every one to get up and say his morning prayers and begin the work of the day. All over Cairo are found these Mohammedan places of worship, and from their towers and minarets, five times a day, the muezzin's call to prayer serves the people for a town clock.

"Thou must put on thy best clothes to-day," said Nabul's mother, as she opened a low wooden box painted green with red and gold decorations. This was Nabul's own particular trunk, and from it was taken his best suit. Instead of the blue cotton gown which Nabul usually wore, he to-day put on a white one that had pretty yellow silk stripes in it, tying it in with a broad red silk sash at his waist. After this he stuck his little turban jauntily on the side of his head so that its long black tassel hung right down over one eye, but he did not seem to mind this in the least.

"There will not be another donkey boy in Cairo as fine as thee," said little Zaida, clapping her hands, while Menah stuffed in her brother's pocket a piece of sweet bread and some dates wrapped in a handkerchief for his lunch. Nor did she forget a couple of morsels of sugar for Teddy Pasha.

Nabul now rushed down-stairs to the stable, the Pasha neighing good morning to him as he heard his little master come in the door. Nabul brushed and rubbed the little donkey down until his coat was as fine and glossy as a little donkey's coat could be. Then he dusted off the gaily coloured blanket and threw it over Teddy Pasha's back, and strapped on the high padded red saddle, after which, catching the bridle, hung with red tassels and little bells in his hand, he sprang on his back, Teddy looking back at his little master and wiggling his ears as though he quite approved of everything that had been done.

"Now be off, little dove, we are fine enough for the Khedive himself," said Nabul, waving a good-bye with his stick to the home folks, and riding away to join Abdal, who was just then leading his donkey out of its stable door near by.

"Art thou ready?" cried Nabul as he came up to his cousin. Abdal nodded and mounted quickly, and away went the two boys laughing and shouting and calling out pet names to their donkeys as they galloped along.

Soon the boys had left the narrow winding streets of old Cairo behind them, and were trotting past the beautiful gardens and through the wide thoroughfares where are only the fine modern houses and big hotels. Finally they halted in front of the great hotel where the strangers were staying.

Early as it was, there was a crowd of natives standing on the sidewalk and gathered about the steps leading from the broad terrace to the street. All of them were hoping to attract the attention of the guests of the hotel, some of whom were already eating their breakfasts at little tables set about on the terrace.

There were beggars of all sorts asking alms, and street peddlers with their wares well displayed. Some of these were loaded down with heavy rugs and draperies, others had their arms full of gold and silver embroideries, or tinsel knickknacks of all kinds. There were snake-charmers and musicians and jugglers too. It was like a circus or a county fair. There were the dragomans, as the guides are called, in a group all by themselves, looking as if they owned the earth, as they swaggered grandly up and down the pavement dressed in their handsome silk clothes. No wonder they felt proud, for they were a big, fine-looking lot of fellows, and most of them spoke many languages. Our two little friends looked at them with admiration, for you must know it is the ambition of every donkey boy to become a dragoman himself some day.

In spite of the haste of our little friends, there were already other donkey boys ahead of them. These were gathered about a tall dragoman who stood leaning against the railings smoking his cigarette and paying not a bit of attention to them.

"There is Mustapha, the dragoman," whispered Nabul to his friend, pointing to the group; "he too has on his beautiful new clothes."

"Yes, and see how those other fellows stick close to him, like flies around a honey jar," answered Abdal.

"Aha! they well know that Mustapha is the most popular dragoman in Cairo, and they hope that he will hire their donkeys," answered Nabul.

Our two little friends now slipped off their donkeys and ran up to the big dragoman, crying, "We are here, oh, Mustapha! send away these others."

This made the other boys clamour all the louder. Meanwhile Mustapha paid not the slightest attention to any of them, but went on puffing away at his cigarette, for Egyptians have the bad habit of smoking one of these nasty little cigarettes at nearly all times.

Mustapha did indeed look gorgeous. He had on a bright green silk garment and over this a pale yellow silk gown; a rich red sash was wound round his waist many times and around his head was rolled the folds of a great silken turban of white and gold.

"Thou will want us, oh, Mustapha?" questioned Nabul at last in a whisper, giving Mustapha's sleeve a tug to remind the great man that they were still there.

"Who can tell? Allah alone knows the mind of these strangers," answered the dragoman, finally. "It may be that they will even want to ride in one of those evil-smelling flying carriages," he continued, throwing a scornful glance at a big automobile that just at that moment came to a halt beside them, one of the few to be seen in Egypt.

It is true that there are even automobiles in Egypt, and every dragoman and donkey boy is very jealous of them, for they are afraid that if there are too many automobiles, people will not ride on their camels and donkeys.

"Who would not rather ride on a beautiful donkey like mine than in one of those noisy, smelly things?" said Abdal, patting his little donkey's head.

"Hush, here come the two strangers," whispered Abdal, as a little boy, followed by a tall gentleman, came out on to the terrace.

But Mustapha's quick eye had seen them, and forgetting his lofty manners he tossed away his cigarette and was smiling and bowing down to the ground when the little American boy ran up to him, crying: "Here is our dragoman, isn't he splendid, and look at all the little donkeys! Oh, do let us take a donkey ride right now, Uncle Ben," he went on eagerly, "wouldn't that be lots of fun, so much better than tramping about as we did yesterday?"

"Well, it's the thing to do when one comes to Egypt, so perhaps we had better try it if you think I can find a donkey high enough to keep my feet off the ground," said the tall gentleman, looking the little donkeys over.

All the donkey boys saw that he was talking about them, and pressed eagerly around, waving their sticks wildly, and each calling out that his was the best and fastest donkey in Cairo, and there was no other like him in all the world.

Little Nabul, with his arm over the Pasha's neck, called out as loudly as any of them, but his heart sank when he saw the little American put his hand on the bridle of one of the other donkeys standing near him. What chance had he among so many big fellows? And suppose Mustapha forgot his promise, after all! Mustapha was so busy talking to the tall gentleman that he paid no attention to the boys.

At that moment a big donkey boy pushed Nabul so roughly to one side that both he and Teddy Pasha came very near tumbling between the long legs of a great wobbly camel that was just coming down the street laden with big sacks of grain hung across the humps on his back.

"You ought to be ashamed of yourself to hit a little fellow like that," cried the little American boy, who had seen it all. "You are twice as big as he."

Meanwhile Nabul had recovered his balance with tears of anger and mortification in his eyes. His pretty suit was splashed with mud, and the end of the rough, heavy sack that was slung across the camel's back had badly scratched the Pasha's saddle. With his heart almost bursting with grief and rage he went at the big boy with Abdal close behind him. If he could only give him a good whack with his stick!

"That's right, go for him," shouted the little American excitedly, rushing down the steps, "I'll help you out!" For a minute it looked as if there would be a general fight, but Mustapha with great dignity got between the boys and talked so sternly in Arabic to the big one that he was glad enough to slink away to the farther side of the street, glad indeed that he had not got the beating which he deserved.

"Never mind," said the little American to Nabul, "I will ride your donkey. I think he is the nicest of them all, anyway."

Nabul did not understand all he said, but he knew what he meant quickly enough.

"Oh, yes," he cried, "me speak American, too."

"Oh, can you? Then we can talk together and we shall understand each other very well," cried the little American with great joy.

Nabul was so happy that he could only grin and point to the Pasha. "Teddy Pasha, his name, Teddy Pasha," he kept on saying.

"Oh, Uncle Ben, his little donkey is named Teddy; we must have him now, mustn't we?" cried George, as our little American friend was named.

"I don't imagine he can talk very much 'American' as he calls it," replied Uncle Ben, "but Mustapha has just been telling me that these two boys are good reliable little fellows and advises us to take them."

"I am sure they are," said George, enthusiastically, who had already made friends with the Pasha.

"Well, so long as you have made up your mind to see Egypt on donkey back, and are going to make your staid old uncle do the same thing, we will try these two boys and their donkeys to-day, and if they suit us we will engage them for the whole time we are here," said his uncle.

"Oh, you will be sure to like it, Uncle Ben," said George coaxingly; but he well knew that his uncle would do anything to please him, even to riding on a jolting donkey over the rough streets of Cairo.

CHAPTER II

A DONKEY RIDE AROUND CAIRO

AFTER it was all arranged, and Nabul and Abdal were actually sure that they were to be hired, they were so happy that they did not know whether they were standing on their heads or heels.

"Well, mount your steed, George, and we will be off," said the tall gentleman, George's uncle, Mr. Benjamin Winthrop. Mr. Winthrop had already mounted Abdal's donkey, hunching up his knees so that his feet would not touch the ground, so George clambered up on Teddy Pasha's high red saddle and the little donkey started off at a lively trot without waiting for a tap from Nabul's stick. Away went the little party down the street, the two Egyptian boys running along, each by the side of his donkey, crying out so as to clear the road ahead, and every now and again giving the donkeys a gentle stroke with their sticks, not to make them go faster, but to guide them. They gave them first a tap on one side and then on the other, as they wanted them to go to the left or right.

"My! but they bounce you about," called out George to his uncle. It was the first time he had ever ridden a donkey and he was holding on for dear life for fear he would be shaken off.

"These Egyptian donkeys have got a funny sort of trot, but it's all right when you once get used to it," said Uncle Ben. "It's a bit rough at first, but just sit easy and you will soon swing into the motion."

So George tried to look, at least, as if he felt easy. Now they had left the new part of the city, frequented by the foreigners, behind them, and were entering the old city where only the natives live.

Here the streets are so narrow that often the roofs of houses nearly meet overhead, and they are so cluttered up that it is a wonder that any one can pass along. There were no sidewalks and everybody walked in the middle of the street. All the people who had any work to do seemed to be doing it in the middle of the street, instead of in their houses.

The donkeys soon had to slacken their pace, for there was a perfect tangle of people and donkeys and little carts, and even a two-horse carriage tried to push through occasionally. This gave George a chance to breathe easier, and watch the process by which Nabul guided the Pasha through the crowd.

"Keep to the right, oh, my lord!" Nabul cried out to a richly dressed man who was crossing the street. "Look to the left of you, oh, my mother," he yelled to an old woman who was bending under a great basket of bread. Little Egyptian children usually call old women and men by some such respectful names as "Mother" or "Father" or "My Lord." They know well how to address their elders.

Presently there was a great hubbub and everybody made way for two tall, strong fellows dressed in white, with gaudy red and gold embroidered vests and red turbans, who came running down the street shouting as they went. Each carried a long white wand; behind them came a handsome carriage and pair.

"Make way for the syces and the carriage of the great Pasha," cried Nabul, and the little donkeys squeezed up against the side of the house, though even then there was barely room for the carriage to pass.

George wanted to know who syces were. Mustapha, who had accompanied the party, explained that they were the men servants who ran before the carriages of great personages to clear the way for them. They can run all day as fast as horses can trot, and never get weary.

"Don't you ever get tired, either?" asked George of Nabul as he ran along beside him. The little Egyptian boy only laughed and shook his head. It was funny, he thought, how all these strangers asked him the same question when he took them to ride. He thought nothing of running all day long by the side of his donkey. Egyptian children are a strong, hardy little race of people and never seem to know what it is to be tired. They live much in the open air and they sleep on a hard bed, all of which tends to make them healthy and strong.

"Now how on earth are we going to pass through here?" asked George, as they turned a corner and saw a long string of camels coming toward them. Across each camel were slung two great bulging sacks that nearly touched the houses on each side.

"Hi-yah! Hi-yah! Jannib ya hu!" (which meant, "Keep to the side, oh, you!") shrieked Nabul and Abdal to the men who had the camels in charge. But the camels stalked along in the middle of the way, wagging their long necks and, of course, the donkeys had to stop, for there was no room to pass.

Such a clamour as set up! The donkey boys screamed at the camel drivers, and the camel men yelled back at them; while Mustapha sat on his donkey calling the camels and their owners all the names he could think of.

"One would think they were all going to break each other's heads, wouldn't you, Uncle Ben?" said George, beginning to get uneasy.

"It's only their way of settling a difficulty, they have no idea of doing harm to any one," answered Mr. Winthrop. And this was true enough. Egyptians are not as quarrelsome as they seem. Peace was restored shortly, and the camel drivers prodded their camels with their sticks until they squeezed up against one side of the street, leaving just room enough for the donkeys to get past. As it was, the last camel in the line nipped off George's cap and Nabul had to rescue it, but the boys only thought this a good joke.

Now they were trotting through a long covered way on either side of which were tiny shops or booths for the sale of all sorts of wares.

"The Bazaar! the Bazaar where you buy pretty things!" said Nabul, pointing to the little booths where the merchants sat surrounded by all sorts of merchandise, clothes to wear, furniture and dishes to use, and good things to eat.

"So these are what you call stores; they look more like boxes," exclaimed George. "Sha'n't we stop now, Uncle Ben, and look at some of the things?"

"Mustapha says we should go to the great mosque first, and visit the Bazaars after lunch," called back his uncle.

So on went the little donkeys, climbing up into the very oldest part of the city, called the Citadel. Here they clattered through an ancient gateway and soon found themselves in a dark, gloomy street. The little donkeys went slowly now, for it was a steep climb around and around with high walls on either side, until at last they came out at the very top on a sort of terrace, overlooking the city now far below, and there stood the great Mosque of Mohammed-Ali, with its great central dome and slender towers or minarets.

"Isn't it fine?" exclaimed George, as he slipped off the Pasha and stood looking up at the great building.

"Yes, but there are other mosques in Cairo that are much older," answered his uncle, "but this is the most interesting of all to see."

"Alabaster, all alabaster," said Nabul, laying his hand on the stone work near the great entrance.

"Much of the mosque is built of pure white alabaster," explained Mustapha, and indeed it is a fact that it is built of this fine white stone. It shows plainly what good taste these old Mohammedan builders had and what fine workmen they were.

"Can't we go inside?" asked George, starting at once for the door.

"Wait, the babouches," cried Nabul and Abdal together, catching George by the arm and pointing to a big pile of yellow slippers just inside the door. These slippers, or babouches, were in charge of an old man with a long white beard and a dirty gown, and he had as assistants two or three boys who squatted beside the pile of footwear. On seeing the approach of the visitors one of the boys picked out the smallest pair of babouches he could find and motioned to George to put them on over his shoes.

"What is that for?" asked George, bewildered.

"No one can enter a Mohammedan mosque with the shoes in which he walks the street," answered Mustapha. "We Mohammedans leave ours at the door, but for the strangers there are these slippers, or babouches, to be worn over their shoes so that the sacred carpets of the mosque may not be defiled."

George thought it very funny as he stuck his feet into the big, wobbly yellow slippers. Nabul simply shuffled out of his own little red slippers and left them in charge of the boys at the door, whose business it was to guard such footgear while their owners were inside. Meanwhile Abdal stayed behind to guard the donkeys.

They entered a great hall where were many graceful columns, but the place seemed bare, for there were no furnishings of any kind, except that the floor was covered with rich rugs, and from the ceiling hung hundreds of glittering lamps. On one side was a sort of pulpit at the top of a short flight of stairs. There were a number of people saying their prayers in the mosque. They would kneel and bow their heads to the floor and stand up and raise up their arms, all making the motions together. It made George think of the gymnastic exercises in his school at home.

"Nabul, I believe I have lost one of those precious old slippers," said George, suddenly looking down at his feet.

Nabul looked horrified when he saw George with only one slipper on.

"I find," he said, and hurried back the way they had come.

Mustapha turned around to see what was the matter, and waved his arms wildly and jabbered out a string of words when George told him what had happened.

"What do you suppose they will do to me, Uncle Ben," laughed George, "put me in prison? It is not my fault the old slipper came off, it's as big as a boat anyhow."

"I know what would have happened not so very many years ago," answered his uncle. "We should probably all have been mobbed, if not killed, for it is only of recent years that people who are not Mohammedans have been allowed to come inside the mosques at all. There is nothing which shows the character and habits of the natives of Cairo better than by observing how their religion enters into their daily lives."

"It's a regular 'hunt the slipper game,'" said George, as he watched the little Egyptian looking carefully over the rugs.

Suddenly Nabul came running back with something in his clothes.

"Quick, I put him on," he whispered, slipping the missing babouche on George's foot, at the same time glancing around to see that no one was looking. No one was looking, and nothing happened, though George wondered if that would have been the case if he had been found with only one slipper.

At the door they dropped the babouches for good, and outside found Abdal playing games with some boys, and the donkeys fast asleep. They were soon waked up, and our party cantered back to the hotel for lunch, for as George said, "It's funny how seeing things makes you so hungry."

Mustapha told the boys to be back at two o'clock with their donkeys, but just now they were cantering off for their own midday meal. Nabul was in such high spirits that he must stop and buy some hot fried peppers and a pile of sticky sweet cakes from the man who sat under a big red umbrella frying big red and green peppers in a pan of olive oil which stood on a small brazier of charcoal. It is the custom for the sellers of vegetables and cakes to cook them in the open air in order to attract trade by the odours and sweet smell of the cooking.

The man began to ladle out some of the hot greasy peppers. "More, more, 'tis not enough for a coin like that," cried the boy, throwing down a silver piece with a lofty air.

"Oho, thou eatest like a nobleman to-day," said the old man, peering at the coin. "Since when have the donkey boys become so rich?"

"There is a little American lord at the big hotel, and I am to be his donkey boy," answered Nabul, as he and Abdal carefully divided the peppers between them.

"Umph, yes, for a ride through the Bazaar and back again like all these stranger folk," said the old man as he flung some more peppers in his pan.

The boys only laughed and went off to eat their lunch in company with their companions in the great square.

There were a lot of their comrades there and they hailed our little friends at once, eager to know all about the strangers to whom they had hired out their donkeys, but Nabul and Abdal kept a discreet silence, only hinting that the strangers were doubtless princes in their own country. Donkey boys love to brag, but they are apt to be a jealous lot and are on their guard against any interference from one another.

One by one the boys got tired of asking questions and dozed off curled up on the dusty ground; but the young Egyptians did not mind this; nor the heat, the sun was very hot even though it was in winter; nor the swarm of flies that buzzed around them. But little Nabul could not sleep, he sat there thinking of the little American, and wondering how long he would keep him for his donkey boy.

If he would hire him for a long time what a lot of money he would make, and what a lot of things he could buy with it. He would buy himself a new suit to wear on the last day of Ramadan, the Mohammedans' great religious fête, when everybody who possibly could put on new clothes of the finest stuffs and the brightest colours. He would buy a new saddle for Teddy Pasha, for his present one was looking the least bit shabby, and the scratch that it got from the rough sack on the camel's back that morning had not improved it in the least. The owner of a horse or donkey in Egypt will always dress up his steed as elaborately as his means will allow, and never, never, if it can be helped, will he drive him with a shabby saddle or bridle. Perhaps, even, there would be enough to buy new dresses for the little girls and a pair of silver bracelets for the mother, for all Egyptian women folk are very fond of jewelry. He would like to buy something, too, for the father, but before he knew it Nabul was fast asleep dreaming of untold riches, and only awoke with a jerk when Abdal reached over and shook him into wakefulness, for the sun told them it was time to be at work again.

George was hanging over the railing of the terrace of the hotel on the look-out for them as they came up, and waved his hat in the air when he caught sight of Teddy Pasha again.

This time all started off towards the quarter of the big Bazaars. Here they found many tourists like themselves mounted on donkeys, for everybody who comes to Cairo must take a ride through the Bazaars where there are such curious and beautiful things for sale. All the same, if one was not a mere tourist, and wanted to learn of the manners and customs of the people, these curious streets and squares of little shops were quite the best places in the city to observe how hundreds and thousands of folk gained their living in most strange ways.

It was funny to see the merchants run out and hail the passers-by, and beg them to look at their wares. One shopkeeper nearly lifted Uncle Ben off the donkey, much to George's amusement. Many of them were very polite, too, and offered visitors coffee when they took their seats on the stools in front of a shop. The people in the Bazaar were almost as interesting as the shops themselves. There were the tall Egyptians of the towns and fellaheen from the country and Bedouin Arabs from the desert in their long, flowing white cloaks, and big black people from the Soudan in the far South. Everybody jabbered at once, but all spoke the same speech. It was curious how, looking so different, they were all practically of one race and religion. There were also numbers of Egyptian women all bundled up in black with white veils over their faces, for neither the Egyptian nor Arab women would ever think of allowing a strange man to see their faces.

George had a chance to become better acquainted with the boys while his uncle was making some purchases. He found that not only could they speak a little English, but some French and a few words of Italian, too. The little Egyptian donkey boys are remarkably quick to catch up a foreign language. Nabul told him how he had learned his funny broken English. He had first picked up words from the tourists who rode on his donkey, and Mustapha had taught him a good deal, for he spoke English very well.

Their own speech in Arabic sounds very strange when translated into our own tongue, as the Egyptians, and indeed all the races which speak Arabic, are very fond of using big words, and they invariably express themselves in the most formal and dignified manner. In the evening Nabul had gone to the English school all one year, and really he had acquired so much English that he could chatter away as fast as the little American, if not always so grammatically correct.

So by the time they had ridden through many more quaint streets and the beautiful Esbekiyeh Gardens and were well on their way back the boys were good friends.

"Please do tell them now that we will take them for our donkey boys for all the time we are here, Uncle Ben," George whispered when they alighted once more at the hotel.

"They do seem to be good obliging little fellows, and as you are the one to be pleased, for you will do most of the riding, I will tell Mustapha to arrange it with them," said Mr. Winthrop.

So it was settled that the services of the two boys and their donkeys should be engaged for a month, with the understanding that they would be free to do business with other people if at any time they were not needed.

And weren't the little Egyptians delighted! They cried "Salaam, salaam, O gracious Effendi!" many times, which was their way of saying "Thank you, sir!" They strutted through the usual crowd of donkey boys hanging about, puffed up with pride, and were followed by the envious glances of the other boys, for it was not often one of their number fell in with such a piece of good luck.

And how happy they all were in Nabul's home when he rushed in with the news. The little sisters hugged him and the mother gave him an extra nice supper, and he went to sleep that night dreaming that he was a big, fine dragoman and that Teddy Pasha wore a great red turban and could talk English.

Every morning bright and early Nabul and Abdal with the donkeys, all looking as spick and span as possible, would be waiting in front of the hotel for the little "Effendi," as they called George Winthrop, and when Mr. Winthrop and George were ready away they would ride.

Big, fat Mustapha, jolting up and down on his own donkey, would lead the way, and showed them each day some of the many strange and curious things to be seen in and around the city, until finally George felt quite as much at home in Cairo as did his new found friends.

One day they hurried through lunch to go to see the "Whirling Dervishes," a queer lot of people, who spin around and around like a top, as fast as ever they can, until they are so tired they drop on the floor. They saw the "Howling Dervishes," too, men in gowns of many colours, with wild faces and long hair, whose blood-curdling howls as they swayed themselves to and fro almost frightened George, who could not understand how people could possibly do such queer things as an act of worship. These are only two of the many sects of the Mohammedan religion.

One day they crossed over to the island in the river Nile, where Mustapha knocked at a gate which was opened by a man in a long green gown, and they found themselves in a garden among trees loaded with oranges and lemons. Here George crept behind the boys along the top of a wall to a spot where, so the story runs, the baby Moses was found asleep in his cradle in the bulrushes by a daughter of the Pharaoh. The Pharaohs were the ancient kings of Egypt. It was most interesting for George, who was surprised indeed to find this land of Mohammedanism had recollections also of his own Christian religion.

Another day they all rode out to a place named Heliopolis, where long ago there was a great city called the City of the Sun. Now only a tall granite obelisk stands there, and any little American can see its "twin," as George called it, if he or she will go to New York City and look at the big obelisk which stands in Central Park. Once upon a time several obelisks stood side by side at Heliopolis, but the Khedive, the ruler of Egypt, some years ago wanted to make a valuable present to the United States, so he gave them one of these obelisks, the same which to-day may be seen in New York City.

When they visited the great Museum Uncle Ben and George stood amazed before the great mummy cases and the petrified mummies themselves (many of them the old kings of Egypt), which have been buried for thousands of years, and only recently been brought to light. It is by preserving all these great finds, dug up from the soil often in the most unexpected places, that it has been possible to write the history of Egypt.

CHAPTER III

THE BOYS CLIMB THE PYRAMIDS

"UNCLE Ben, I am going to ride the Pasha out to the Pyramids," announced George, as they were talking over their plans for a trip to the great Pyramids of Gizeh. They had just come in from a ride, and Nabul and Abdal were anxiously waiting, fearful lest the tall Effendi would say, "Well, boys, we won't need you to-morrow."

"Do you really mean to say that when you can either drive in a comfortable automobile or carriage, or ride on a street-car out to the Pyramids, that you prefer donkey back?" asked his uncle.

"Indeed I do, Uncle Ben, it's lots more fun," said George, "besides we can ride in automobiles and street-cars when we are home."

George was now quite used to riding donkey-back, though didn't he feel tired and bumped about the first day or two! But now he could ride as well as the little Egyptian boys, and Nabul had taught him how to guide the donkey by taps with his heels; as for Teddy Pasha, he obeyed George almost as well as he did his little master.

"And Nabul, how will he get out there, run all the way? It's some distance, you know," said Mr. Winthrop, smiling at the boys.

"No, no!" broke in Nabul eagerly, "I ride behind the young Effendi; Teddy Pasha, he is strong."

"Yes, uncle, you know how strong these little donkeys are; they don't mind one bit carrying two persons. When Nabul gets tired of walking he can easily ride behind with me, can't you, Nabul?" chimed in George.

Nabul nodded vigorously, "Yes, yes."

"Well, if you boys and Teddy Pasha don't mind, it's all right," laughed Uncle Ben, "but if you don't object, I am going to drive, so, Abdal, I will not want you to-day, but there is a gentleman in the hotel who wants a donkey boy, and I have told him to take you," continued Mr. Winthrop.

The boys all pulled long faces, especially Abdal, who knew he was going to miss a good time, for they intended to take their lunch and stay the day.

"It is just as well if neither of them went," muttered Mustapha, "there is sure to be trouble with the boys out there."

George started to ask why, but before he had a chance Mustapha carried the boys off to make arrangements for the morrow.

Little Nabul was at his usual place bright and early the next morning, all ready for their trip to the great Pyramids. He had a broad grin on his face as he peered through the railings and "salaamed" or bowed to Mr. Winthrop and George, who were finishing their breakfast at one of the little tables on the terrace.

The Pasha, too, looked around and wriggled his ears knowingly.

"He smells sugar, the rascal," exclaimed George, who had got in the habit of giving him sugar, and so, filling his pocket from the sugar-bowl, he came down into the street and began feeding it to the donkey.

Mustapha now came up with a small open carriage, and they got off at once, leaving Abdal looking very blue.

Uncle Ben was in the carriage and Mustapha on the seat beside the driver, while George on Teddy Pasha trotted along, guided by Nabul on foot as usual.

Soon they were crossing the bridge across the Nile which has two great stone lions at either end, and then out on to a long, straight avenue shaded by big trees, which leads straight as an arrow from the city of Cairo out to the Pyramids.

There were many people coming and going along the great avenue. The country folks were bringing their produce into the city to sell, and much of it was carried on the backs of donkeys. There were great lumbering carts drawn by oxen, and long lines of camels, laden with such big loads piled on their backs that they looked like moving mountains.

Up to the very gates of Cairo come the great gardens and farms which grow bountiful supplies of vegetables and fruits, and there are even great wheat-fields watered by the flowing Nile and tilled by the fellaheen, or labourers, after the same manner that the natives of Arabia, across the Red Sea, worked in Bible times.

Egypt is a great and progressive and very wealthy country, but the country folk have not all been taught as yet how to get the best results from their labour. They are learning rapidly, however, and they see things in the city, when they bring their produce to market, which please their fancies, and now in many an Egyptian farmhouse built of sun-baked mud, and even in the tents of the Bedouin Arabs of the desert, one often sees those common nickel alarm clocks, oil lamps, and even little hand sewing-machines.

Amidst all this throng of country people going citywards our friends made but slow progress. Often the little donkeys from the country would pass, carrying two and sometimes three big men on their backs.

"See what great loads these country donkeys have to carry," said Nabul to his donkey. "Thou shouldst be willing to carry me for a while," and so saying Nabul jumped up on Teddy Pasha's broad back behind the little American.

Teddy Pasha turned his head around with an inquiring look as much as to say, "Oh, yes, I can see you," and then drooped his ears, then stood stock-still. Not a foot would he budge.

"Go on, lazy one, is this the way that thou wilt disgrace me?" cried Nabul, beating his heels against the Pasha. "No one will again believe me when I praise thee! Oh, thou ungrateful beast!" he continued, half-crying with vexation. By this time the carriage was far ahead and some little children wading in a pool by the wayside began to jeer at them.

George remembered the sugar in his pocket and tried to coax the Pasha with some of it. The Pasha ate it gratefully, but that was all he would do.

At this moment the boys heard some one laugh behind them, and the jingle of donkey bells, and who should go dashing past them but Abdal on his donkey, Bobs!

The minute Pasha saw it was Bobs passing him he got on his mettle and away he went after him. Meantime the carriage had halted, and when the boys came up, Uncle Ben was looking anxiously around and Mustapha was ready to scold.

"Why dost thou linger?" he demanded of Nabul, "and Abdal, why art thou not in the city earning money instead of galloping all over the country?"

"I knew well that when the Effendi reaches the great Pyramids he will want to ride out to see the wonderful Sphinx, and I knew, too, he would not want to ride one of those miserable little donkeys that one finds there, so, behold, I am here at his service," and Abdal, quite unabashed, smiled so sweetly at Mr. Winthrop, that the gentleman did not have the heart to scold him for deserting his friend at the hotel.

"Thou wilt have to fight, then, with the donkey boys at the Pyramids; they will call thee a meddler, and perhaps beat thee," called out Mustapha ungraciously as the little procession started on again.

"Pouf," said Nabul, "they are only Bedouins." The little boys who live in Cairo have a great contempt for the Bedouins, the people who live in the desert.

"Why should they object to our riding your donkeys?" asked George, full of curiosity.

Nabul explained in his broken English that there was a tribe of Bedouins who lived near the Pyramids, who thought that they only had the right to act as guides to the visitors who come to see these great monuments. This was because the men of their tribe had been doing this for years and years; and it was thus that they resented any one coming in and interfering with their ancient privileges.

"I call that real selfish, don't you, Uncle Ben?" exclaimed George.

"But they shall not fight me and Abdal, we are your donkey boys; you ride our donkeys in the great city, and you shall ride our donkeys at the Pyramids; it is the same thing; they shall not run us away," said little Nabul stoutly.

"We won't let them," declared George, and he doubled up his fists, "we'll fight first."

"Behold the great Pyramids!" called out Mustapha, pointing between the trees. Sure enough, there stood the three Pyramids, that every child knows so well from the pictures, rising one behind the other.

"They look very small," said George disappointedly.

"But they are big, very big, wait and you will see," said Nabul. This was quite true. As they rode nearer, the Pyramids seemed to grow bigger and bigger. Now as they had come to the end of the avenue the carriage stopped, for only the sandy desert lay beyond.

Abdal had Bobs ready and Uncle Ben mounted, and away they went up a sloping hill toward the largest of the three Pyramids. All around the base of this Pyramid were gathered a crowd of Egyptians, men and boys, leading camels and donkeys. As soon as they caught sight of the little party, this howling crowd came rushing to meet them. A number of them gathered around Uncle Ben and George, catching hold of them; shouting in their own language and in broken English, "Take me for guide! Take me for guide!" Such a din as they kept up was never heard anywhere else.

George did not know whether to laugh or to feel frightened when two big fellows tried to pull him off his donkey, but he held on to Teddy Pasha for dear life, and the Pasha helped him fend off the fellows by backing his ears and kicking out with his heels.

Meanwhile Nabul and Abdal were brandishing their sticks in the faces of the Bedouins and calling them all kinds of names, all the while holding on tightly to the bridles of their own donkeys. Big, fat Mustapha forgot all about his dignity and went at the fellows, trying to push them away and shouting at the top of his voice. In the midst of the fuss Nabul cried out: "O Sheik, O Sheik, decide for us!" At the same time he rushed up to a tall man with a long gray beard and flowing white garments, who strode up, giving the crowd of Bedouins a whack first to one side and then to the other with a high staff which he carried in his hand.

"Oh, thou ruffians, wilt thou drive the strangers away with thy violence?" demanded the old man, looking sternly around him, while Mustapha explained things to him.

"The Sheik will make them behave now," said Abdal.

"How can he?" asked George, glad to be free of the two Bedouins who had been pestering him.

"It is the Sheik of the Pyramids, the chief of the tribe, they must obey him," answered Nabul.

"Who gave them the right to guard the Pyramids? Why can't anybody walk around here alone if he wants to?" persisted the American boy.

"I know not, it has always been so," said Nabul with a shrug of his shoulders.

"Ah! And they pay many pieces of gold as a tax for the right," chimed in Abdal, looking wise.

"They rob the travellers of money, too, the thieves!" returned Nabul, glowering at a bunch of donkey boys who were poking all manner of fun at the little boys from the city, though they did not dare to attack them while the Sheik was around.

Mustapha had evidently arranged matters with the Sheik, and came back with four of the Bedouins whom he said would take Mr. Winthrop and George up to the top of the great Pyramid.

"Dear me, I certainly don't need two big men to help me climb up there," exclaimed George. "Why, it must be as easy as can be to climb from one of those steps to another, Uncle Ben."

"It's probably harder work than it looks, just try it," answered his uncle.

Mustapha was going to sit in the shade and have a friendly smoke with the Sheik, and rest after his exertions, but he very graciously told Nabul and Abdal that, if they wanted to, they could leave their donkeys in his charge and climb up with the "young Effendi."

Nothing loath, the little Egyptians began to scramble up the side of the great Pyramid, calling to George to follow, that they knew the way.

The Pyramids are so built that the stones form great steps from the bottom to the top. To George's great surprise when he got to the first of these steps, which looked so small from the ground, he found it was as high as he was. The little Egyptian boys quickly hoisted themselves up, and nothing daunted, George followed as best he could; but after two or three of these high steps, he was glad enough to have his two guides take hold of his arms—one on either side—and lift him easily from one big step to the other. George was so out of breath that he could not say a word, but only watch Nabul and Abdal away ahead of him, climbing up the great stone blocks like gazelles. The ascent seemed to take a long time to George, but it was really only a few minutes before the two Bedouins lifted him over the last step. Close behind him came his uncle, panting between his two guides, and the little party now found themselves on a sort of platform at the tip-top of the great Pyramid.

How much could be seen from their lofty perch! And how eager were the little Egyptians to point out everything to the strangers!

There were the other two Pyramids, much smaller than the one they stood on, which is called the Pyramid of Cheops. On one side stretched the great yellow desert of sand and rocks; on the other were green fields and groups of little Arab villages and palm-trees. That silver ribbon running through the green fields, way off yonder, was the great waterway of the Nile, and there beside it was the big white city of Cairo. They laughed as they looked down on the guides and donkey boys far below, for they looked like little toy figures.

"The Pyramids were built for tombs, weren't they, Uncle Ben?" asked George, as they rested and sipped tiny cups of coffee, which they bought from a man dressed in a yellow gown and green turban who sat beside a small brazier of charcoal making coffee to sell to the visitors.

"Yes, by those old Kings of Egypt—the Pharaohs. The stones of which they are built were brought from great distances and put into place by regular armies of men who worked many long years. Even to-day there is more or less mystery surrounding them, and strangers from all over the world never cease to wonder and marvel at these curious monuments."

After resting awhile, our party climbed down again, which was almost as hard work as getting up. At the bottom the donkey boys of the Pyramids were waiting for them again, and only the Sheik's stern eye kept them in good order.

"You see that door there," said Nabul, pointing to an opening in the base of the Pyramid; "you can go inside if you like. It is said that the great kings of olden times were buried in there. That is the door to the tombs; and there is a great room inside with pictures painted on the walls, but oh, it is dark, I like it not," said little Nabul, shaking his head.

George did not think he would like it, either, and wanted to know where the Sphinx was. So all mounted the donkeys again and trotted through the sand to see the Sphinx, followed by the disappointed Bedouin donkey boys who finally one by one trailed off and left them in peace.

"I thought the Sphinx was right beside the Pyramids. I don't see it now," said George.

"It is there, the great Sphinx, see!" said Nabul, as they turned around a hillock of sand. Sure enough there was the big stone head sticking up out of the sand. Nabul and Abdal brought the donkeys to a standstill in front of it, and the boys stood on the edge of a great pit staring at the strange figure which has the head of a human being and the body of a lion, and which was carved out of the rock so long ago that no one now knows its history.

"Look, the Sphinx smiles, she always smiles like that," whispered Nabul (he called it "Spinkie" in a funny little way). "I think sometimes I can see her mouth move." It is quite true that the stone lips do seem to smile.

"Let's climb up and whisper something in its ear," said George. The boys ran down the sloping sides of the great pit in which sat the Sphinx, but to George's amazement he found that he could not even climb up to one of the great paws, much less the head which towered high above them.

By this time they all decided that they were very hungry, and that it would be a fine idea to have a picnic between the paws of the great Sphinx. So Mustapha opened the lunch basket which he had brought, and the little party seated themselves in the shade of the strange stone face, and spread out the contents of the palm-leaf basket on a big flat stone. Nabul and Abdal had their lunch stowed away somewhere in their garments, and they were eager that George should taste their favourite dish of fried peppers that—ugh!—made his mouth smart, though he liked their sweet honey cakes. But not for anything would the little Egyptian boys eat any of the nice cold ham which was a part of his lunch, for no little Mohammedan child, or grown person either, would touch pork in any shape or form. It was against their religion.

Then they discovered that they were very thirsty, and Abdal ran off to find something cool to drink, and came back with one of the vendors of lemonade who hang around the Pyramids selling their cool drinks. The sherbutli, as Abdal called him, wore a bright red apron and carried little blue china cups on a brass tray. These he filled with lemonade from the big glass bottle which was slung over his shoulder, and the children thought nothing ever tasted nicer.

They rested for awhile and amused themselves watching the people who came riding up on camels or donkeys to see the Sphinx. Finally Mustapha said it was time to go back to the city, and though George stoutly declared he wasn't a bit tired he was not really sorry when Uncle Ben said that he had better drive back in the carriage with him, and Teddy Pasha and Bobs were probably glad, too, when they turned into their stables that night.

CHAPTER IV

BEN HASSAN'S DAHABEAH

NABUL often talked with the "little Effendi" during their rides together, of his home and the mother and the two little sisters, and about his father and the dahabeah with its huge sails, until nothing would do but George must know them all and take a trip on the dahabeah.

The boys had their heads together a lot these days, and at last it came out that it would be a splendid plan for all of them to take a trip up the Nile on the dahabeah of Nabul's father.

"Think what a treat it will be, Uncle Ben," said George, "to go and live on a real Egyptian boat. Nabul's mother is going to keep house for us on board, and the little girls will help her. Then, just think! we can take the donkeys, too," continued George, warming up more and more to his subject.

"Well! George, you seem to have thought of everything," and Mr. Winthrop laughed long and heartily. "I did not know you had such a head for business. It does not seem a bad idea, however, this river trip of yours; there must be much that is interesting to be seen in that way," continued his uncle. "I will ask Mustapha what he thinks about it."

"Uncle Ben, you are a good fellow!" exclaimed George, jumping up and hugging his uncle, for now he would have a chance to see something of the real life of the country such as the tourists who stayed only in the cities never had.

Mustapha was very bland and gracious when he found out that he was expected to go along, too. He said that Ben Hassan, Nabul's father, was a good friend of his, that there was no more skilful captain nor better dahabeah on the Nile than his, and that everything could be arranged as they wished.

Nabul was a happy little boy the day he guided these wonderful Americans, as he always thought of them, to his home. There they met Nabul's father, a tall, grave man of few words. While he and Uncle Ben talked the trip over (with Mustapha as interpreter, though Ben Hassan knew some English), Mizram the mother gave them coffee served in tiny cups without handles, each set in a brass holder,—the thick Turkish coffee which is all grounds and sugar which one gets in Egypt. Then the two little sisters crept in to see the kind people their brother had talked so much about. Menah, who was the eldest, was rather shy and quiet, but Zaida was a roguish, merry little soul who made friends easily. They did not know a word of English, but by smiles and gestures they made friends with George and showed him all their treasures. There was the big white cockatoo who swung on his perch and could talk, and a cage of small singing birds that Abdal's father had sent them.

And the little girls had some dolls of which they were very proud. The dolls were queer little figures, fashioned after those which had been dug up from old tombs where they had been buried for centuries. There were odd little stone and clay figures, too, which the girls treasured quite as much as they did the dolls in human form. One was in the form of a Nile crocodile, another of a buffalo and another of a lion, and still others in the form of goats, camels, and donkeys. There was another doll in the form of a man carrying a great basket on his shoulder and another of a washerwoman.

The custom of little Egyptian children playing with these dolls and figures is very old—for all the world their dolls are like the Noah's Ark animals which you have at home—and ages and ages ago, when little children died, their dolls were always buried with them.

After the call upon Nabul's family everybody trooped down to the river to see the Isis, which was the name of Ben Hassan's dahabeah, and Mr. Winthrop agreed with George that it was just the thing they would both like, so it was all arranged on the spot without further ado, and it was decided that they would start on the voyage up-river the following week.

Finally the day came to set sail. It was indeed a busy morning for the family of Ben Hassan! Baskets and pots and pans and jars and sacks of clothing and household belongings of all kinds were loaded on to Teddy Pasha and Bobs, who must have wondered to themselves what was going to happen. At last everything had been thought of, Nabul's mother gave the last directions to the friends whom Abdal lived with who were to look after the house and the fowls and the birds while they were away, then amid good-byes from the neighbours, who were all at their windows and doors to see them off, the little procession started down to the river landing where lay the dahabeah.

"Hurry up, lazy one," cried Abdal, "thou wilt have plenty of time to rest," as he hurried Bobs along with a tap from his stick.

"Thou dost not go that way to-day," said Nabul, giving Teddy Pasha's bridle a jerk as he started to turn down his habitual street. "Thou goest on a longer journey to-day." And the two little donkeys put their heads together as if to discuss this unusual proceeding.

When they got to the dahabeah everybody was bustling about, putting the boat in order for the voyage. Nabul's father was standing on the little upper deck giving orders to some of the crew who were looking to the ropes and sails, while others were scrubbing the deck. Here and there were piled up all sorts of things, gaily painted wooden boxes, which are the kind of trunks Egyptians use, baskets of eatables, live chickens, and big water-jars.

Everybody was talking and shouting all at once in the usual Egyptian fashion. Mizram, however, at once set to work to get things straightened out, and the little girls helped her as best they could.

In the midst of it all the carriage drove up with Mr. Winthrop and George and their baggage, with Mustapha beside the driver. George was standing up waving his cap, and was out of the carriage before it stopped. He rushed up the gang-plank and on to the deck, and insisted on shaking hands with everybody, beginning with the reis, as a Nile captain is named, and ending with the boy washing down the deck. Every one was greatly surprised, for Egyptians don't known anything about shaking hands in our way. Their ceremonies of politeness are quite as marked, but very different, as, for instance, a kiss on the forehead.

Meanwhile Mustapha was in his element, storming about and calling on the great Prophet Mohammed to bear witness that they would never be able to get off with such a crew of dullards.

"As for me I am going to get out of the way by going on the upper deck, it seems to be the only quiet place on board," said Uncle Ben, as he dodged the chickens and took refuge on the elevated stern of the boat where the grave, stately reis gave him a deep salaam of welcome.

Urged on by Mustapha's threats, the little crew soon began to get things in order. The tug of war came when it was time for the donkeys to come aboard. The boys got them up to the plank, but there they just planted their feet down firmly and not another step would they budge. They weren't going to leave dry land. Nabul coaxed and pulled, and Abdal clucked and prodded, but all Teddy Pasha did was to back his ears and give an awful bray, which made the crowd of loafers gathered on the river bank laugh. Finally Nabul tied a cloth over the Pasha's head, and while he pulled hard at the bridle in front Abdal tweaked the little donkey's tail, and this made him so mad that he dashed up the plank and on to the deck before he knew it, and just as soon as Bobs saw him go he rushed aft. The donkeys were then led triumphantly to their quarters in the prow of the boat, where they were very comfortable and content. George at once christened this part of the boat "the menagerie," for the chickens were already there pecking away at some grain, each fastened to the railing by a long string tied around one leg to keep them from flying overboard. The little girls, too, had brought the big white cockatoo to keep them company, and his wooden cage hung against the side of the cabin, while curled up in a tight box was a tame snake belonging to one of the crew. The Egyptians of all ages and all classes are very fond of pets.

George was as excited and happy as could be as he rushed about with the children from one end of the boat to the other.

"Isn't it funny to see sailors in long white gowns and turbans on their heads, Uncle Ben?" laughed George. "How can they ever climb up the rigging in clothes like that?"

"But they don't have any rigging to climb, on a dahabeah, they only have to shift a rope once and again," said Mr. Winthrop.

There was a large sail in the bow and a much smaller one in the stern, each of them of the great pointed lateen variety seen on the rivers and along the coasts of all Mediterranean countries. The boat itself was a sharp-prowed, broad-bottomed affair which seemed to glide over the water rather than through it. The Nile dahabeahs are among the most picturesque boats afloat.

In the stern, on the lower deck, were two small cabins for Uncle Ben and George, and a little saloon to eat in. Further forward was the kitchen and storeroom, and beyond these the quarters for the reis's family and Mustapha.

"We sleep on the deck," said Nabul. "Abdal and I just roll up in a blanket and lie down on the deck boards, and sleep just like the crew."

"I should like to do that, too; it must be lots more fun than sleeping in a stuffy little cabin," exclaimed George, much interested.

"It's hard if you aren't used to it, but we think nothing of doing so," said Abdal.

At last the friends who had come down to see them off had taken their leave, and the gang-plank was drawn in, the sails unfurled, and two of the men seized a couple of big oars and pushed off the prow from the bank. Slowly the dahabeah swung over to the middle of the stream; the crowd on shore shouted a last farewell; the breeze caught and filled the big sails, and in a few minutes they were gliding swiftly through the muddy brown water of the Nile, up river toward the very heart of the "dark continent" of Africa.

On the upper deck Mustapha had just put two long wicker chairs for the "Effendis," and Uncle Ben, who had picked up a little Arabic, was comfortably stretched out in one trying to talk with the reis, who sat beside him on a rug spread on the deck smoking his big "hubble-bubble" pipe, every once in awhile giving an order to one of the crew as they trimmed the sails to catch all the breeze.

Mats were spread on the decks for the others; the children, however, were too busy to think of sitting down; they kept running from one side to the other, watching the houses and people on the banks as they slipped past, and the queer craft going and coming on the river.

"There come three nuggars," said Abdal, pointing to three broad, flat, barge-like boats, each with a high lateen sail, coming slowly toward them.

"What a funny name! what are 'nuggars'?" asked George.

"Nuggars are the great Nile cargo boats which carry all kinds of merchandise up and down the river," said Nabul. "See the great boxes and bales on that one," he continued.

"And the one behind has a lot of oxen and sheep on it; they are loaded down to the water's edge, I wonder they don't sink," said George. "Oh! And here come three haystacks floating down-stream! With sails on top of them, too!" he cried.

But no, they too were boats, this time loaded with fodder and the long green bamboos which were being carried to the city. Then a ferryboat filled with people and donkeys crossed the river ahead of them, rowed by men in dark blue cotton gowns. It was all so novel and amusing the children were almost sorry to stop looking in order to eat lunch, though George did say he was hungry enough to eat a hippopotamus.

One of the men brought a table and noiselessly set it on deck for the "Effendis," and then served them the nice things that Mizram had cooked. There was chicken with a nice hot pepper sauce and rice and all kinds of vegetables and melons and dates and oranges.

At the other end of the deck the reis and his family and Mustapha had their meal. Mizram served them all sorts of queer dishes that the little Egyptians kept on bringing to the "Effendi" to taste; and how they laughed at the faces the little American made over some of them!

"'After Al-Ghada, rest, if it be but for two moments;

After Al-Asha, walk, if it be but two steps,'"

said Mustapha, quoting one of their proverbs as he stretched himself on a rug for a nap after dinner. Al-Ghada is dinner and Al-Asha is supper.

"Nabul, what is in that bag?" asked George, pointing to a big brown bag which hung on the side of the mast of the dahabeah, and which one of the men was just taking down.

"It is the food of the crew. They put it there so that all can see it and no one can steal any of it without his fellows seeing him. The crew are going to eat their dinner now," explained Nabul, "and that fellow there has just climbed up and unhooked it."

By this time the sun was beating down hotly on the canvas awning over the deck, and one by one everybody followed Mustapha's advice, except the men on duty. The little Egyptian children, curled up on their mats, were soon sound asleep. George stoutly declared that he was not going to miss anything by sleeping. Mr. Winthrop had brought a book that told all about Egypt, and George listened while his uncle read aloud about Memphis, which they would soon pass. Thousands of years ago it had been another burial-place, when the haughty Pharaohs reigned in Egypt. But the first thing that George knew, he had forgotten all about the Pharaohs, and woke with a start in his big chair by the rattle of the sails as they were dropped, while the dahabeah gently glided to the landing-place, where the reis was to deliver some merchandise which he had brought up to a dweller on the bank from a Cairo dealer in ironware.

From the landing-place on the river the party had time to take a ride inland, and Nabul and Abdal had the donkeys all ready as soon as the gangplank was pushed out. There was no trouble in getting the little donkeys off the boat. The minute they saw the dry land they made a dash for the shore. And weren't the donkey boys on the landing mad when they saw that the strangers had brought their own donkeys. They howled and shouted, and wanted to know how the Cairo donkeys could be expected to carry the visitors through the sand and rough soil hereabouts.

However, they felt better when Mustapha picked out two of their donkeys,—one for himself and the other for the two little girls,—grumbling at the same time something about "too many children," but as Nabul whispered to Abdal, "Mustapha was like an old camel with a hard mouth and a soft heart."

The little girls were wild with delight that they were going, too. Menah sat with her feet hanging over one side and Zaida behind her with her feet dangling down the other side of the little donkey.

Away went the little procession, the donkeys kicking up a cloud of dust. The road wound through fields of grain, and along the roadside were to be seen children guarding cows and goats and other animals, who shouted merry greetings to our little friends as they passed by.

It was not long before Mustapha, who was riding ahead, called out, "Now you can see the village, there between the palms," at the same time pointing with his cane—which a dragoman is never without—to a large grove of palm-trees they were approaching and amongst which were huddled a lot of queer flat-roofed houses.

"I don't see anything but big stones," said George.

"Let's see who gets there first," cried Nabul; and giving the donkeys a tap away the boys raced, the Pasha being the first to come to a halt beside the palm-trees.

"Now I can see that one of the stones is a house, Uncle Ben," cried George as they drew up closer.

There were some natives standing on the little landing of the minaret of the mosque, which no village hereabouts is without, whether it be large or small, and the children lost no time in following their example and climbing up the crazy stairs which wound around inside the slim tower.

The view round about was wonderfully varied. On one side stretched away the sandy desert, where the Bedouin shepherds guarded their flocks of goats, leading them from one little oasis to another, wherever they could find enough herbage to make a meal. On the other side was the flowering river-bottom of the Nile, one of the richest agricultural regions in the world.

Just beside the mosque was a great grove of date palms, and George thought it very strange, and very much to his liking, too, that he could reach out his hand just beyond the gallery railing and pick the golden dates. "How I should like to come up here every day," he said as they made their way down to the ground.

Just before the entrance to the mosque was a great stone statue which astonished George and his uncle very much. The natives, too, evidently had a great regard for it, as they had planted a lot of low-growing, flowering trees all about it, sheltering it as if it were in a bower.

"How long do you suppose it has been here, Uncle Ben?" asked George, as he took his seat on the broad foot of the big statue.

"A long, long time, certainly, my boy," replied his uncle, "perhaps thousands of years."

After admiring the great statue awhile longer they discovered Mustapha sitting on the shady terrace of a coffee shop. He was drinking another of those little cups of muddy-looking, sweetish Turkish coffee of which the Egyptians are so fond. Uncle Ben, too, liked it very much, for it was usually made of the purest of Mocha coffee which comes from the other side of the Red Sea not far away from Egypt, so he too stopped for a cup, the boys meanwhile wandering off with the little girls quite by themselves.

When they all got back to the coffee shop again each of the children had a little wicker cage or basket in which was imprisoned a chameleon, a queer little beast like a lizard, which lives by catching flies and insects.

The Egyptians have a superstition that to have a chameleon in the house is almost as good as having a cat—and they are very fond of cats, too. The cat catches rats and mice and the chameleon gathers in all the stinging bugs and insects and flies. This chameleon is thus a very useful little animal indeed. When frightened it changes the colour of its skin instantaneously in a most remarkable manner. It takes on quite a different colour from what it had a moment before. If it is lying on a green leaf it becomes a green colour so like the leaf it can hardly be seen, or if on the yellow sand or a gray stone it becomes yellow or gray in turn. The children had bought the chameleons for a few small coins from some native boys whose acquaintance they had made in their stroll about the village.

Mustapha finally called out that they must go on if they wanted to get back to the boat before dark.

The next morning George was awakened at daybreak by a funny sort of singing and a great clucking of poultry. He dressed himself quickly and ran out on deck. The crew had cast off from the moorings, and as the big sail was being hoisted the sailors sang a slow, monotonous chant with the words, "Pray, pray to Mohammed!" as a sort of chorus. In a few minutes the dahabeah was again under way.

From the "menagerie" still came a clucking of distressed hens, a snorting and braying of donkeys, mingled with the shouts of children.

"What can be the matter?" thought George as he hurried to the forward end of the boat.

There a funny sight met his eyes! The pet snake had, by some means or other, wriggled itself out between the slats of its box during the night and eaten one of the hens, and now lay gorged and drowsy on the deck, raising its head occasionally to give a feeble hiss at the other chickens, who were clucking and fluttering about at the ends of their cords, frightened out of what few wits a chicken has.

Nabul and Abdal were doing their best to pacify the donkeys, who showed that they didn't like snakes either, by trying to back over the side of the boat.

The cockatoo was swinging on his perch with every feather standing on end, while Menah and Zaida stood huddled together on top of a box, though they knew that the snake could not bite as his fangs had been taken out.

In the middle of the commotion was Mustapha, angrily scolding the sailor who owned the snake and who was cringing and bowing before the dragoman, making all sorts of excuses for his snake.

"Do we buy fowls to feed thy snake?" demanded Mustapha angrily. "Thou shalt pay the price of the chicken."

"Indeed, it was a fine fat hen and cost several piastres," put in Mizram.

The sailor meanwhile was putting the sleepy snake back into its box, calling it an "ingrate" and a "heartless viper" for thus causing its master so much trouble.

"What a lot of talk over one chicken," laughed George when he was telling his uncle about it. But this is just the way these people go on over small things.

When things quieted down breakfast was served on deck, after which the children hung on the railings and enjoyed watching the many things of interest on the shores as the strong northerly breeze carried the dahabeah swiftly along. Sometimes they passed so near the shore that they could call to the little brown children paddling along the water's edge, who would answer back greetings, and hold out their hands and call out, "Backsheesh, give us backsheesh," which meant they wanted pennies thrown to them.

Menah and Zaida were much interested in a group of girls who had brought their big copper pots and water-jars down to the edge of the river, and were scrubbing them while they chatted together, after which they would fill the jars with water and balancing them on their heads go gaily singing back to their homes.

"See the fisherman yonder, he is about to throw his net," cried Abdal, pointing to a man who stood on the high bank with a large net gathered up in his arms. With a swing of his arms the man skilfully flung the net out into the river. It spread out into a great circle as it touched the water. The boys explained to George how it was weighted with stones, and as it slowly sank to the bottom it would imprison the fish so they could not get away. One has to be very skilful to do that, they said.

Sometimes the children would all gather around Mustapha and listen to his wonderful tales. How when he was young he took long journeys on camel-back far south in the great Lybian Desert, which they could see stretching away on their right. Once, too, he had there killed a lion which had chased him, and there were still lions to be found there, but not so many as there used to be. When he told them how he had seen crocodiles basking in the sun on the river banks, not so very far from Cairo, the children clapped their hands and wanted to know if they weren't going to see some crocodiles.

"And hippopotamuses, too?" asked George. But Mustapha shook his head and said he thought not, that there was so much traffic and so many steamboats and other craft on the river now that these animals had been frightened away and were only found now in the Upper Nile, far beyond where they were going. This disappointed the boys very much.

Then again to while away the time the little Egyptians would show George how to play their games, while George in turn would attempt to teach them some of the American children's games.

On several occasions the sailor brought his tame snake on the upper deck and showed them all the wonderful tricks his pet could do. The snake would follow him all around the deck, holding its head erect and waving it about as if it liked the queer little tune the man whistled. The sailor offered to let the snake wrap itself around the boys' arms, but they would not agree to this, though they thought it amusing enough to watch its tricks with its master.

Everybody was so much amused by the snake's tricks that Mustapha amiably told the sailor he would not have to pay for the chicken it had eaten.

Abdal had been telling the "little Effendi" so much about his home in the country that George was anxious to see an Egyptian farm.

So the boys talked it over with Mustapha, and as the farm was not far from the river Mustapha said it would be possible to stop off there for a day or so on their way back.

Mustapha then busied himself all one day writing a letter to Abdal's father, saying that he and his party would stop at his farm and telling him what day the dahabeah would be at his landing, that he might make preparations to welcome the American Effendis.

George wondered how Mustapha was going to send the letter, but just then a big "steam dahabeah" passed them coming down the river crowded with a lot of tourists. The reis said this was their chance to send back Mustapha's letter. So he hailed it and as it slowed down he ordered several of his crew to launch the small boat which the dahabeah carried. This they did, and rowing over to the steamer threw the letter on board as she steamed past them. So George thought there was some use after all for a steamboat on the Nile, though it did seem out of place and not at all as comfortable and picturesque way of travelling as by a sailing vessel.

It was always a great event for the children when the boat was tied up near some little village in order to lay in a new stock of provisions, to get some grain to carry further on, or to deliver some which they had brought from Cairo. They would all go on shore and it was great fun watching the people who came from near-by farms bringing vegetables and fruits and fowls to sell. They crowded around Mustapha, who did the bargaining, shouting in a high voice the prices of their wares. At each landing they always found the water-sellers who refilled the big water-jars on board, from the goat-skin water-bags slung by a strap over their shoulders. All the little children came trooping down from the neighbouring villages to stare shyly at the strangers, often hiding half-afraid behind their mother's gowns; but whether they were shy or bold, all of them would hold out their hands for backsheesh; even the babies perched on their mothers' shoulders held out their little hands, though they could not speak a word.

"'Tis the strangers who have spoiled them," Mustapha said as he drove away a crowd of little children who were pestering George at one little village. "They throw coins to the little ones on the banks as they go past on the great steamers; they mean it kindly, but it teaches our little Egyptian children to beg and that makes them bad," and the fat dragoman scowled at the village children until they shook in their little slippers and ran away as fast as possible.

As they went farther up the river the green fields grew fewer and fewer and the yellow sand of the deserts on both sides came nearer and nearer the river.

One morning the Isis rounded a sharp bend in the river and there in the distance were a group of tall columns, rising from the bank surrounded by houses and trees.

"'Tis Luxor, the site of the most wonderful ruins in all Egypt," said Mustapha with pride.

Everybody crowded eagerly forward while Mustapha pointed out the places of interest. First came the part of the town where the Egyptians live and then the great hotels and gay shops, and finally, just at noon, our dahabeah pushed its high prow in among a lot of other dahabeahs and smaller craft, and tied up alongside the old temple with its row of a hundred tall columns which towered high above them on the river bank.

CHAPTER V

AN EGYPTIAN FARM

THE little folks and the donkeys as well were wild to get on shore again and stretch their legs a bit, for they had not left the boat for several days. As soon as they could get away from the boat they scampered off past the big hotels where many tourists were sitting on the verandas and in the gardens sipping cool drinks just as they did at Cairo.

Everywhere George and his uncle were followed around by people who wanted to sell them relics which they said they had found in the ancient ruins,—coins and scarabs and pottery, and all sorts of odd things. Mustapha waved them all away. "Their antiquities are only make-believes," he said, with contempt. "There are people who make these imitations, and these fellows make a business by selling them to travellers as real curiosities. Sometimes there were real treasures that could be picked up at a bargain, but not so many as in the old days," said Mustapha.

Sun-up next morning found our little party riding out on another excursion. Mizram had packed many good things to eat in a big palm-leaf basket covered over with green leaves to keep the things cool, and this was slung across Teddy Pasha's broad back. Our friends were to have a picnic among some riverside ruins.

Soon they were riding between two rows of stone figures; an avenue of Sphinxes, like the great Sphinx at the Pyramids, only much smaller, and in a few minutes more all dismounted at the entrance to a great temple.

Such a rabble surrounded them! Beggars clamouring for backsheesh, people wanting to guide them through the ruins, and vendors of relics. Mustapha and the boys had to use their sticks freely to make the crowd stand back.

Two donkey boys promised to look after the donkeys, so after threatening them with all sorts of dire punishments if any harm should come to their animals, Nabul and his cousin ran after their little American friend.

For several hours Mustapha led his little band in and out among the great columns and across the broad courts of ancient temples. There seemed to be thousands of these columns, some standing in long rows, others lying broken on the ground. How the children stared at the pictures painted on the walls by the old Egyptians, the colours as fresh as if they had just been painted. Mustapha showed them how these pictures made a regular story-book, if one only knew how to read them. Here were a lot of pictures that told all about the doings of one of the Pharaohs,—how he went to war and the battles he fought. There were other pictures showing how he went hunting, and the various kinds of animals and birds he had brought back with him from the chase.

The children thought it was most amusing to read a story-book like that, and went about trying to make up stories for themselves out of the pictures.

They stopped to watch a number of men hard at work among the ruins lifting a fallen stone column. More than three hundred Egyptians were working to set up the fallen columns and clear away the rubbish, and they worked in much the same way as did the ancient Egyptians who built the same temples. There were many young boys, too, helping to pull on the long ropes by which the columns were raised.

"Come, let us hunt and perhaps we can find some relics for ourselves," said Nabul. "One of the donkey boys last year found a little statue."

"I would like to find a mummy," exclaimed George, as the boys went to work prodding in the sand with their sticks.

"Mummies are too heavy to carry away," said Abdal, wisely shaking his head.

"I should like to find a doll," whispered Menah to her sister as they too turned over the sand in their little fingers, thinking of her own curious little dolls at home fashioned after the same manner as those frequently found among the ruins. "You remember the great traveller who went with our father in the dahabeah to some old city? How he had many men to dig in the sand for him, and how they found many wonderful things there? Well, he said that often the dolls and toys that were put in a little girl's tomb would be made of gold and silver," replied Menah. "I should like a doll of real gold to play with."

Pretty soon the children tired of their search and stretched themselves out in the shade of an enormous stone column to rest.

Our party made many excursions to see many other old ruins, and one day Mustapha took them to see some funny camel races. It was the queerest thing in the world to see the long-legged camels come swinging along, covering yards and yards of ground at each step, each camel ridden by an Arab in flowing white dress and head covering. After this there was a race among the donkey boys. Nabul and Abdal were wild to join in this, but found it was against the rules for outsiders to enter.

"They are jealous, they know we could beat these up-country donkeys," Nabul consoled himself with saying, but he hurrahed with everybody else all the same when a lively little gray donkey, ridden by a small boy in a green dress, reached the goal first and got the prize.

One morning early found the Isis again sailing up the river toward Assouan and the Great Cataract, which was to be their last stopping-place.

When George and Uncle Ben arrived at Assouan it was market-day, and the square by the riverside was filled with all sorts of queer people and things.

For centuries lower Egypt had been periodically flooded and then dried out again, and the poor native farmers and fellaheen had suffered greatly, many, many thousands even dying of starvation. All the great volume of water in the river Nile became at certain seasons a mere trickling rivulet.

In late years a plan whereby all lower Egypt was to be properly watered and drained has made even the poorest of the labourers of the countryside happy and prosperous. This great benefit was brought about by the building of a great dam just above Assouan, and as the water was let through little by little in the dry season, and properly stored up when it flowed in abundance, it proved to be just the treatment that was needed to make an otherwise suffering people quite contented with their lot.

"I want to see the great Assouan dam," said George one morning as he and Uncle Ben were just finishing their breakfast. George was a most inquiring little fellow, and he had heard some men talking of this great work at the hotel, and he wanted to see for himself what it really was.

George had become so expert with donkeys, that Uncle Ben called him his little donkey boy. Soon all was ready and Mustapha headed the little procession that made its way quickly along through clouds of dust and began struggling over a stony desert road.

Little Menah was riding behind George and Mustapha had been gracious enough to let Zaida sit behind him. The reason of this was that the donkey boys on the quay, who were a lot of wild young fellows from the desert, had come to blows among themselves as to which of their number should go with our party to supply the two extra donkeys required, whereupon Mustapha said he wouldn't have any of them, that they were a set of black heathens anyway,—for some were little negro boys from the Soudan,—so he borrowed a donkey from a friend of his for himself, and divided up the party in this way.

Mustapha was so big and fat and his donkey so small that poor little Zaida had scarcely any room to sit comfortably. George could hear Menah shaking with laughter at her sister's efforts to keep from slipping off at every bounce the donkey gave.

Meanwhile Mustapha, quite unconscious that they were amused at him, was gravely telling them that the high wall of bricks which followed their road was the old-time boundary to Egypt and was built to keep back the hordes of barbarians from the south, but now Egypt was a much greater country and went far beyond this wall.

Soon they came into a little village on the bank of the river which spread out here like a lake. The children laughed when they dismounted and looked at each other. They were so covered with dust that the brown little Egyptians looked white. They shouted and clapped their hands with glee when Mustapha told them to get into a big boat painted with the brightest colours. Six tall black Soudanese, dressed in white, with red fezes, pulled at the oars, keeping time to a queer sort of chant. The children were so busy watching the rowers that, before they knew it, they were gliding past a tiny temple that seemed to be rising out of the water.

"This is the ancient temple of Philæ, one of the most beautiful in Egypt," said Mustapha. "It is on an island, but since the great dam of Assouan was built the island itself is covered by water, and if the dam is raised still higher, as they talk of doing, the little temple will be entirely covered with water, or perhaps destroyed, which would be a pity."

On arriving at the great dam they got into another boat which took them over the First Cataract, or waterfall, on the Nile. Not over the worst part of it by any means, but quite "scary" enough for the little girls. Shortly after they were again back at Assouan.

George would have liked to have kept on up the river to the city of Khartoum, where there is a great school or college erected as a memorial to General Gordon, who opened up and first introduced outside civilization into these parts, but their plans would not permit of spending the extra time. To-day this magnificent school is filled with intelligent, hard-working Egyptian boys who, when they leave college and go out among their fellows, do much to benefit and lift them from the ignorance and superstition which formerly existed.

So the Isis was headed for home, and the good dahabeah raced along, borne by the strong current of the river, as if it knew it was on its way home. The happy days passed quickly and our little friends had many adventures of which there is not time to tell you.

As they came to the wide fertile country above Cairo, and neared Abdal's home, the children were on a sharp lookout, and Abdal was wondering who would come down to the river to meet them. When the Isis did run her sharp prow into the bulrushes at the little landing-place for the farm of Abdal's father, where Mustapha proposed to stop, not only were all of Mustapha's friends there, but most of the villagers besides, and they all gave the visitors the heartiest of welcomes. There was Abdal's father and mother and the baby, and his little brother, who kissed him on both cheeks, and each in turn took the hand of each visitor, kissing his own hand at the same time, a pretty little custom among these people.

After the actual landing Uncle Ben and George mounted the donkeys, and followed by the others on foot, all talking and in the highest spirits, they rode for some distance through great fields of cotton and rice until they came to a little village nestled away in the midst of palm-trees.

Here they stopped at Abdal's father's house, which was the biggest in the village, for Ali-Hijaz was the chief man of the little village and had many "fellaheen," or labourers, working in his cotton, rice, and cane fields.

Ali-Hijaz's house, like all the houses in the village, was built of mud bricks, which had first been baked by the sun; it was thatched with palm-leaves, and the trunks of palm-trees strengthened the walls and formed the rafters. Their host invited them into a large room, where they all seated themselves on mats spread on the hard earthen floor. While Ali-Hijaz offered Mr. Winthrop a long-stemmed pipe to smoke, Abdal and Nabul ran to the little Arab café of the village and soon came back bringing a big metal tray on which were a number of small cups and tiny tin pots of coffee. This was put in the middle of the floor and each person was served with a cup and one of the little pots of coffee. Menah and Zaida amused themselves playing with the baby, while their two mothers gossiped together, and George made friends with Abdal's little brother Amad, whom he thought looked very cunning in his white cotton gown and little turban stuck on his clean-shaven head.

"Just think, Uncle Ben," laughed George, "he can barely walk and yet he goes to the village school at five o'clock in the morning and stays till sundown, only coming home for dinner in the middle of the day. Whew! but that's hard work!"

"And then, all he learns is to recite the Koran—the Mohammedan Bible—at the top of his voice," replied Mr. Winthrop.

"That little mite!" said George with a mock groan. "Well, I am glad I go to school in America."

But Amad seemed to grow fat in spite of it, and was at the head of the procession when the children trooped out to see the village. All the houses looked alike, with only one big wooden door and no windows, just little slits in the walls for air and light. Within most of these houses there was no furniture of any kind, save some rugs, mats, and cooking utensils, and a few boxes made of the wood of the palm-tree, in which to keep the family clothes. Abdal's father had two European beds in his house which he had brought from Cairo, but the villagers had no use for such new-fangled things. As they walked along all the little village children ran out to talk to Abdal and followed them until, as Nabul said, the procession looked like a kite with a long tail. There were almost as many dogs as children, and George fought rather shy of the fierce-looking mongrel curs that barked at their heels.

Abdal took them into the fields where there was a "sakiyeh," or water-wheel, by which the fields are watered. A lazy-looking old camel was slowly turning a great creaking wooden wheel, and this turned another wheel on the rim of which were fastened a lot of earthen jars. These jars were filled with water as the wheel went down into a sort of well, and as it came up the water from the jars was emptied into a ditch which carried it over the fields in every direction.

Here for the first time George saw a camel ploughing, and such a funny plough it was! Just a log of wood with a pointed iron tip at one end and an upright pole at the other, by which the ploughman could guide it.

When they got back to the home at sunset they found Ali-Hijaz had persuaded Mr. Winthrop to stay a day or two, as there was some good bird shooting in his rice fields, a sportof which Uncle Ben was very fond. This pleased the children, and that evening they had lots of fun playing one of their games called "Playing Pasha." They elected a "Pasha," and the choice fell on George, whom they put in a kind of litter made of palm branches. Four of their number carried this on their shoulders while the rest ran beside carrying lighted wisps of straw and hay for make-believe torches. One of the boys meanwhile beat a drum, and another played a small flute; and thus they marched around the village until the torches were all burned out and their mothers called them to bed.

The two guests were made comfortable in one of the beds, which were only kept for grand occasions like this, and early the next morning Mr. Winthrop and his host, with Mustapha, were off to shoot rice birds.

"We will go and see the wild pigeons," said Abdal, as the boys wondered how they should amuse themselves. "I know where there are many of them roosting in the trees."

"Good," answered Nabul, clapping his hands, and the boys started off across the fields. The Egyptian folk are very fond of the wild pigeons of the country, and like to catch them and keep them for pets.

At the same time many of the Egyptian boys, too, are so cruel as to hunt these gentle birds, killing them with stones which they throw with unerring aim.

"Hist! they roost here," whispered Abdal as they came to a clump of low trees. Just then a number of pigeons flew out of the trees; at the same time, to the great surprise of the boys, one apparently was injured, and fell to the ground, and Nabul ran to pick it up. Some one had evidently injured its leg or wing. Just then two wild, savage-looking young boys came dashing up to Nabul crying, "Thou hast killed one of our tame pigeons, our father shall beat thee," trying at the same time to snatch the bird away from Nabul.

"'Tis not true," returned Nabul angrily, "dost thou think I am such a dullard as not to know a wild pigeon from a tame one?"

"And I know these birds well, I have often been here, they always roost in these trees," exclaimed Abdal. "I know thee, and I know that thy pigeons are far from here."

The Egyptians in the country usually tame many of these pigeons, and build them little houses to live in on the side of their own, and sometimes one will see a big mud tower in the village where hundreds of these pigeons live and build their nests.

In the midst of the dispute a tall man with an ugly, scowling face strode up with a stick, so, thinking things were getting too hot for them, our little friends turned and fled toward the village, Nabul, however, triumphantly holding on to the pigeon.

The other hunting party had brought back a big bag of birds and were well pleased with the day's work.

The next day they were to take leave of their kind hosts and go back to the Isis. When George awakened in the early morning, such a wailing met his ears he could only imagine that some one must be dead. Throwing on his clothes he rushed down the short flight of steps that led from his room to the big room on the ground floor and from there into the yard. There he saw Nabul lying face downward on the ground beside the stable door, with his sisters sitting beside him rocking themselves backwards and forwards and wailing piteously, while Abdal and the older people rushed wildly about all talking at once.

"What is the matter? Nabul, are you hurt?" cried George, rushing up to the little group.

"Teddy Pasha is gone, some thief has stolen him," they all cried in one breath.

It was only too true, the little donkey had mysteriously disappeared in the night. Nabul had got up early to get the Pasha ready for their return to the boat. He had found the little donkey gone, as well as his bridle and saddle; Nabul had been looking for him ever since and had just come back broken-hearted.

"Oh, Nabul, we are sure to find him! Come and we will all look," cried George, nearly ready to cry himself,—he had grown really attached to his little steed.

Poor little Nabul lifted up a wobegone face and slowly rose to his feet. His donkey was like a brother to him, and he felt he would never see him again.

No one thought of going back to the boat until the little donkey was found, and the whole village turned out to search for him.

Suddenly Nabul struck his forehead with his hand. "I know now! Those two ruffian boys we saw yesterday! 'Tis they who have stolen my donkey. The wretches! This is their revenge! We will go to their house and demand news of the Pasha," cried the distracted little boy.

"Follow, I know the way," said Abdal. The boys hurried through the fields and rice swamps until they came to a tumbled-down group of mud huts. No one was in sight save an ugly-looking brute of a dog and a little girl, who peered at the strangers from behind a corner of a wall.

Nabul boldly went up and shook the heavy wooden door of the house and called loudly, but it was tightly fastened and no one answered. He then gave the whistle he always used to call Teddy Pasha, but only the dog began to bark.

George was for battering in the door, but the boys said it was no use. "Teddy is not here, or he would have answered me," sighed Nabul, as he turned away sorrowfully, "but they have stolen him, I am sure."

"They would not dare keep him here so near our village," replied Abdal. "They have doubtless put him in some hiding-place far off. That is their sister," he continued, pointing to the little girl behind the wall. "Where art thy brothers?" he demanded, but she only laughed and made a face at them.

"She knows something," said George, making a face in return at the child. But there was nothing for them to do but walk away and keep on with their search.

At sundown the boys returned home and poor Nabul sat on the ground with his head buried in his arms, refusing to be consoled. He had eaten nothing all day, and when his mother brought him a nice dish of curds she had made herself, he only shook his head.

It was a miserable household and nobody slept much that night. George and Abdal refused to go to bed at all and sat beside Nabul in the big room. Just as George was dozing away at daybreak he was roused up by a terrible bray just outside the door, answered by one from Bobs in the stable.

Like a flash Nabul, who had heard it too, tore open the house door and nearly tumbled over Teddy Pasha, who calmly walked into the middle of the room and stood there as much as to say, "Here I am, at last."

Little Nabul gave a shriek of joy and threw his arms about the little donkey's neck and cried and laughed in the same breath. Abdal called out the good news, and in another moment everybody was petting Teddy Pasha and making as much to-do over him as if he were a long-lost member of the family. As for the little American, he was as happy as could be to see the little companion of his wanderings once more.

But the poor little donkey, wasn't he a sight, all covered with mud! He had evidently been taken away and hidden in the rice swamps; his pretty bridle and saddle were gone, and only a dirty and knotted piece of rope was around his neck. An ugly cut on one of his feet showed where he had been hobbled; his captors had evidently done everything to keep him secure, but in spite of it he had broken away by some means or other, and had come straight back to his master.

After leaving Abdal's family, and just as our party were going on board the dahabeah, Nabul picked up an odd greenish pebble. "What a funny looking stone!" he said. "It looks just like a beetle."

"That is what the learned ones call a scarab,—don't you know there are many of these in the big museum at Cairo?" cried Abdal, as the children bent over the tiny stone.

"Oh! maybe it is old," exclaimed George eagerly, "and worth lots and lots of money."

Just at that moment a party of learned looking men, Europeans, came up the bank from their dahabeah which had tied up just below the Isis. At their head was a Frenchman, an inspector of the Egyptian public monuments. With his party he was going some miles inland to pass judgment upon some newly discovered ruins of which he had recently heard.

"Let us go and ask the great Frenchman, he surely can tell us," and so saying, Nabul ran back to where Mr. Winthrop and the Frenchman were already talking together.

"Please, monsieur, is this old?" said Nabul, in his queer French, holding up the little pebble carved in the form of the sacred beetle of the Egyptians.

"Eh!" said the great man, taking the beetle in his hand. "Is it old, indeed!" he exclaimed in great excitement. "It is a sacred scarab. Most rare! There are only two others like it in the world. Where did you find it, mon petit?"

Nabul pointed out the spot where he had found the stone.

"Voila! and to think that I have already passed over that spot and did not know one of the most ancient and most wonderful scarabs known to the world was lying there!" and the great man paced up and down, running his hands through his hair.

"Mon petit," the Frenchman said at last, stopping in front of Nabul, "you know the great museum at Cairo? Well, if you will take this little stone to the gentleman who is in charge there, he will be very glad to have it, and the authorities of the museum will reward you handsomely; it is worth more than money to them. I will give you a letter, which you must also give to this gentleman," and so saying the Frenchman took a pencil out of his pocket, and, tearing a leaf out of a small blank book, quickly wrote a few words and gave it to Nabul. "I will write him myself at once," he continued, "but I beg of you to guard the scarab most carefully. I rely on you to see that he does not lose it," said the Frenchman, turning earnestly to Mr. Winthrop. "It does not seem fair to take it from him unless I at once took it myself to Cairo, and it is impossible for me to leave here now."

Mr. Winthrop and all of them promised, for they were all now interested in the wonderful stone, and Nabul proudly and carefully hid it inside his embroidered vest.

There was a happy little party on the dahabeah when she set sail again, and many were the farewells to the kind people of the little village, who all came to see them off.

And wasn't Teddy Pasha a spoiled and pampered little donkey! He was petted and fed and rubbed down by everybody on board until he not only looked as fine and sleek as ever, but also got so fat and lazy that Mustapha doubted if he would ever be willing to do any more work.

At last the Isis floated up to her moorings at Cairo, and everybody felt that they were home again. The first thing George did was to buy the finest donkey saddle and bridle he could find in Cairo and give to Teddy Pasha, who thereupon got vainer than ever. George and his little

Egyptian friends took many more rides together before he and Uncle Ben went back to America. They all went together when Nabul carried the wonderful scarab and the Frenchman's letter to the great man in the big museum, who talked very wisely about it. He thanked Nabul and told him he had done his country a service, and used a lot of long words that the children could not understand. But one day, not long afterward, a man in a fine uniform came riding in great style up to Nabul's house and gave little Nabul a sealed packet from the authorities of the big museum, and in it was a handsome sum of money for the little donkey boy who found the wonderful scarab.

It was enough indeed to set him up as a dragoman when he was older, but this would not be, Nabul promised himself, until he had first made a visit to see his little friend, George, in that wonderful country over the sea.

And thus it happened that the Little American Cousin really did bring the good fortune to little Nabul, the youngest donkey boy in the big city of Cairo.

THE END.